# The New Puppy

## Catherine and Laurence Anholt

ORCHARD BOOKS

For Claire, who loves dogs

Orchard Books
96 Leonard Street, London EC2A 4XD
*Orchard Books, Australia*
14 Mars Road, Lane Cove, NSW 2066
First published in Great Britain in 1994
This edition published in 1999
ISBN 1 84121 347 0 (hardback)
ISBN 1 84121 055 2 (paperback)
Text © Laurence Anholt 1994
Illustrations © Catherine Anholt 1994
The rights of Laurence Anholt to be identified as the author and
Catherine Anholt to be identified as the illustrator have been
asserted by them in accordance with the
Copyright, Designs and Patents Act, 1988.
A CIP catalogue record for this book is available from the British Library
1 3 5 7 9 10 8 6 4 2 (hardback)
5 7 9 10 8 6 4 (paperback)
Printed in Belgium

Anna loved dogs.

She had china dogs and clockwork dogs,

fluffy dogs and bedtime dogs.

She had pictures of dogs on her bedroom wall.

She even had a pair of black and white doggy slippers.

She had every kind you could think of except . . . a real dog!

Sometimes Anna would pretend her little
brother was a dog.  She taught him to
bark and crawl around the floor.
Then she patted him and gave
him a biscuit. "Good boy,"
said Anna.

But it wasn't the same.  Anna wanted a real dog.

Her dad wasn't so sure.

"A puppy needs to be looked after and trained," he said.

"I could help," said Anna.

"It would eat a lot of food and need exercise."

"I could do that too," she said.

"It wouldn't stay little for long."

"I like big dogs," said Anna.

"You couldn't just change your mind and get rid of it."

"I know," said Anna, "it'll be one of the family!"

Wherever she went, Anna looked at dogs. She tried to decide which kind she'd like. Some were

too long

too tall

too loud

too sleepy

too neat

too hairy

too huge

too small

too spotty

and some were just too silly.

One day Anna and her dad went for a walk in the countryside. They saw a field full of sheep and a farmer with a black and white dog.

Suddenly the dog ran across the field and began chasing the sheep through a gate.

"Look at that naughty dog!" said Anna.

"That's not a naughty dog," said the farmer, "that's my sheep dog. She helps me on the farm."

"I wouldn't mind a dog like that,"
said Anna's dad.

"Well, come and look in here," said the farmer, opening the
door of a shed.

Inside were six of the sweetest puppies Anna had ever seen.
The farmer told Anna their names:

Teeny

Tiny

Tony

Topsy

Tiger

and Tess.

"They will all need a home," said the farmer.

"Well, I think we could give one of them a good home,
don't you Anna?" said her dad.

Anna didn't know which one to choose.  They were all so
lovely.  Then one of the puppies chose her!  The roundest,
fattest, happiest of them all waddled across and licked Anna
right on her nose.

"That's Tess," laughed the farmer.  "I think she likes you."
"Yes," smiled Anna, "and I like her.  You'll be one of the
family, won't you, Tess?"

Tess was still too small to leave
her mother, so Anna had to
wait a few weeks.

It seemed like a long time but Anna and her brother got
everything ready. They found a bowl and put an old
blanket in a cardboard box.

WELCOME TES2

At last the day came. Anna and her dad brought the
puppy home.

At first Tess slept most of the time.  She ate lots of
warm food and made puddles on the kitchen floor but
everybody loved her.

Then she started chewing things . . .

her blanket and her cardboard box,

the washing-up gloves and the carpet,

the plants and even Anna's brother.

"Naughty dog!" said Anna, holding her chewed school book.
"You can't eat the whole world!"

Anna and her dad went to the pet shop to buy a proper
bed for Tess and something that she *could* chew.

# There were all kinds of interesting things for dogs :

collars

leads

toys

whistles

biscuits

bones

combs

brushes

shampoo

vitamins

rings and even little coats.

It took them a long time to choose a big red basket and a squeaky teddy, but when they came home, Tess wasn't there!

They searched everywhere. At last, Anna found Tess . . .
in her bedroom.  She was wagging her tail and looking very
pleased with herself.

Tess had chewed everything!
Anna ran downstairs in tears
holding the pieces of her
favourite doggy slippers.

"I DON'T WANT THAT DOG!" she shouted.

"She's only a tiny puppy," reminded her dad, "and she's a long way from her mummy."

But Anna was still very cross at bedtime.

In the middle of the night, she woke up. She thought someone was crying, but her brother was fast asleep.

She tiptoed downstairs and there was Tess, all sad and shivery.

Anna unwrapped the squeaky teddy and gave it to her.

"I'm sorry I shouted at you," she whispered. "I'll be your mummy now."

When Anna's dad came down for breakfast, he found Anna and Tess fast asleep in the new red basket.

Tess didn't stay tiny for long.

She grew

and grew

and GREW

and soon she *was* one of the family.

Anna loves dogs,

china dogs and clockwork dogs,
fluffy dogs and bedtime dogs.

She has every kind you could think of, she even has a pair
of very chewed doggy slippers. But best of all, Anna has . . .

. . . a real dog!